The Mummy Mystery

by
Justin Spelvin

illustrated by
Dave Aikins

SCHOLASTIC INC.

New York Toronto London Auckland Sydney
Mexico City New Delhi Hong Kong Buenos Aires

Archeologists Tyrone, Austin and Uniqua were searching for lost treasures.

But something else was lost too. Or rather, someone.

"Where is Archeologist Pablo?" asked Uniqua.
"I haven't seen him in quite a while," said Austin.
"Uh-oh," said Tyrone.

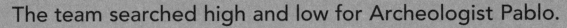

The team searched high and low for Archeologist Pablo.
"Hey, look, guys!" said Uniqua.
"Did you find him?" Austin asked.

"Nope," said Uniqua. "Just this dusty scroll."
"Hey, those look like clues," Austin observed.
"Maybe they'll help us find Pablo!" said
Archeologist Tyrone.

Archeologist Uniqua read the first line. "A ruby sun
shows the way."

"What does that mean?" Austin wondered.

"I don't know," Uniqua replied. "But I found a ruby
this morning!"

As Uniqua held up the stone for the others to see,
a sunbeam blazed through it.

A red arrow appeared in the sand! "Come on, team,"
said Uniqua. "I bet Pablo is that way."

The three archeologists set off in search of their friend.
After a long hot walk, they checked the scroll again.
"What's the next clue?" Archeologist Austin asked.
"Follow the scorpion," Uniqua read aloud.

"No way. Scorpions are dangerous," said Austin.
"Not this one," said Tyrone, pointing to a drawing
in the sand.

Soon the team found themselves at the entrance to a pyramid. They could hear a spooky *OOOoohhhhh* sound coming from inside.

"It's a mummy!" shouted Austin.

"Says who?" asked Tyrone.

"Says the scroll!" said Austin, pointing.

"Well, mummy or no mummy—Pablo might be inside," said Uniqua.

The three brave friends entered the pyramid.

Inside the pyramid, they heard another creepy *OOOoohhhhh* sound. It was closer this time.

"There's nowhere to go," worried
Archeologist Austin.
"What does the scroll say?" asked Tyrone.
"Take the hand of a new friend," Uniqua read.

"A new friend, huh," said Tyrone. "Let's see . . ." He walked over to a statue and clasped its hand.

Sure enough, a secret door opened!

Inside the next room, they heard a *splash*!

"We're close to water!" said Archeologist Uniqua.

"And maybe Pablo!" said Tyrone.

"And maybe the mummy," Austin said, shivering.

They came upon two doors.

Uniqua read the next line on the scroll. "Sometimes right is wrong."

"How can right be wrong?" Austin wondered.

"Easy!" said Tyrone. "When left is right. We need to use the door on the left!"

They walked through the doorway and down a long
corridor—and another—and another.

"I think we're lost," Archeologist Uniqua worried.

"What does the scroll say?" asked Tyrone.

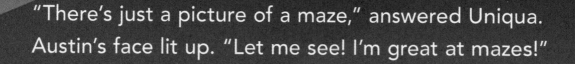

"There's just a picture of a maze," answered Uniqua.
Austin's face lit up. "Let me see! I'm great at mazes!"

He took out a pencil
and got to work.
   "Follow me," he said after a moment.

They followed Archeologist Austin's directions and were out of the maze in no time. "Walk toward the sun," Uniqua read on.

"But we're inside," said Tyrone.

"Look up ahead!" said Austin. At the end of the corridor was a bright light!

The three archeologists walked toward the light. At the end of the hallway they stepped outside and into a . . .

"MUMMY!" they screamed.

"*OOOoohhhhh,*" said the mummy.

"That's not a mummy! That's Archeologist Pablo!" Uniqua shouted.

"Hi guys,"
Pablo said as he
jumped into a big,
beautiful pool. "I'm glad you
found that note I left you. Isn't this place cool?"

"But if you aren't a mummy," Austin asked, "why are you wearing all that cloth?"

"Read the bottom of the scroll," said Pablo.

Uniqua read aloud, "He who stays covered up does not get sunburned."

"Ohhhhhh!" the three archeologists exclaimed. Then they followed Pablo into the cool, blue water.

Nick Jr. Play–to–Learn™ Fundamentals

Skills every child needs, in stories every child will love!

 colors + shapes — Recognizing and identifying basic shapes and colors in the context of a story.

 emotions — Learning to identify and understand a wide range of emotions: happy, sad, excited, frustrated, etc.

imagination — Fostering creative thinking skills through role-play and make-believe.

 **math** — Recognizing early math in the world around us: patterns, shapes, numbers, sequences.

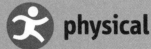 **music + movement** — Celebrating the sounds and rhythms of music and dance.

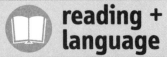 **physical** — Building coordination and confidence through physical activity and play.

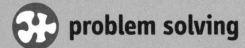 **problem solving** — Using critical thinking skills (observing, listening, following directions) to make predictions and solve problems.

 reading + language — Developing a lifelong love of reading through high interest stories and characters.

 **science** — Fostering curiosity and an interest in the natural world around us.

social skills + cultural diversity — Developing respect for others as unique, interesting people.

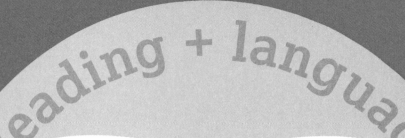

Conversation Spark

Questions and activities for play–to–learn parenting.

Pablo left his friends clues so that they could find him. What kind of clues would you leave? Hide a stuffed animal, then make your own list of clues so that someone can follow them to find it.

For more parent and kid-friendly activities, go to www.nickjr.com.